Petr Horáček

The Mouse
Who Reached
the Sky

To Achille and Aube

First published 2015 by Walker Books Ltd, 87 Vauxhall Walk, London SE11 5HJ

2 4 6 8 10 9 7 5 3 1

This book has been set in WBHoráček

Printed in China

British Library Cataloguing in Publication Data:
a catalogue record for this book is available from the British Library

ISBN 978-1-4063-5822-3

www.walker.co.uk

WALKER BOOKS
AND SUBSIDIARIES
LONDON · BOSTON · SYDNEY · AUCKLAND

But as much
as she tried,

Little Mouse couldn't
reach it by herself.

"I need help," she said.
"I'll go and ask my
friend Mole.

We can play with the
marble together."

"Hello, Mole, are you there?"
called Little Mouse. "I've just seen
a beautiful marble hanging
from the tree!"

"It's red and shiny. If you help me reach
it, we can play with it together!"
"A marble? How exciting!
Of course I'll help," said Mole.

"Silly Mouse," said Mole. "That's not a marble. It's a red, shiny balloon.

We can use it to fly!" Mole stretched and jumped

as high as he could,
but he couldn't reach
it by himself.

"We need more help,"
said Mole.

"Hello, Rabbit," said Little Mouse.
"We've seen a beautiful red balloon in the tree.
If you help us reach it, we can use it to fly!"
"What a great idea," said Rabbit.
"Of course I'll help."

"Silly Mouse and Mole," laughed Rabbit. "That's not a balloon.

It's a big, shiny ball. We can play catch with it!" He stretched and jumped,

but he couldn't
reach it by himself,
either.

"We need someone
taller than me," said Rabbit.
"But no one is that tall!"

"Somebody taller than you?"
shouted Little Mouse.
"I KNOW!"

So Mole climbed
on top of Rabbit and
Little Mouse climbed
on top of Mole.
Together, they
        s t r e t c h e d
and
s t r e t c h e d
and they
wobbled
and
they
wobbled...

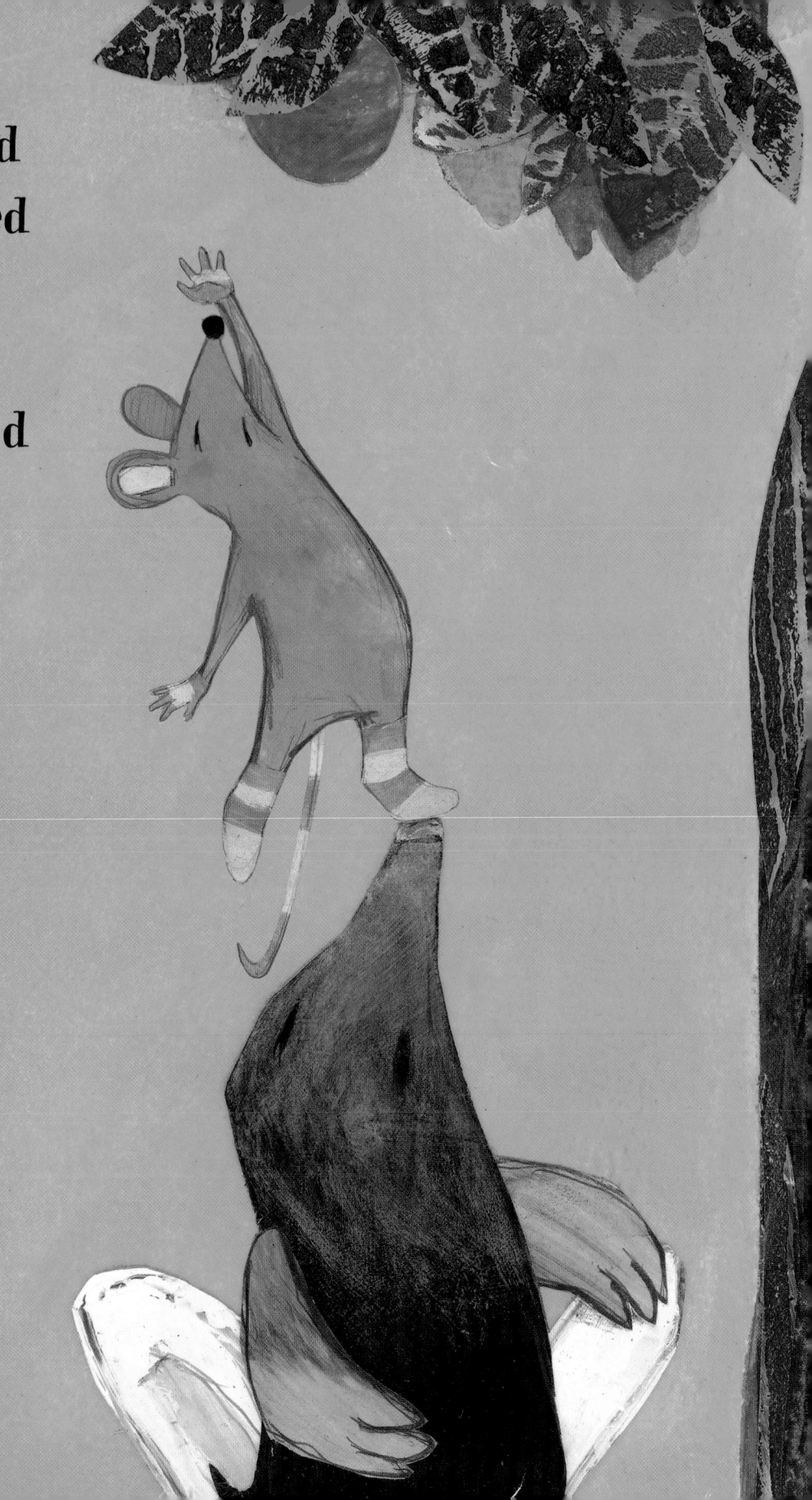

CRASH!

They all fell down!
Little Mouse, Mole and Rabbit
hit the ground so hard that
the tree shook ...

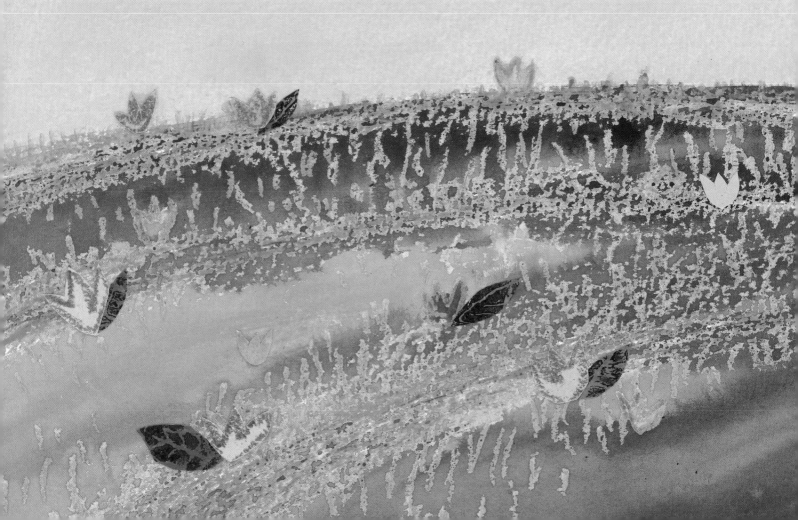

and down came not one,
but hundreds of red, shiny
things!

"Look," said Rabbit, "we've all been silly. It wasn't a marble or a balloon. It wasn't a ball, either! It was a delicious cherry and now we have lots of them to eat."

"Just like magic," said Little Mouse. "Look what we three can do when we help each other!" And they all laughed.